D0008809

ISBN 0 361 08611 3 Hbk
ISBN 0 361 08623 7 Pbk

First published in Great Britain by Purnell Books 1955
This edition published by The Macdonald Group 1990
Orbit House, 1 New Fetter Lane, London, EC4A 1AR

A member of Maxwell Macmillan Pergamon Corporation PLC

Printed and bound in Great Britain by BPCC Paulton Books Ltd
A member of BPCC Ltd

© Darrell Waters
as to the text herein and
The Macdonald Group
as to the artwork herein 1955/1990
All rights reserved

CIP data available from the British Library

NODDY MEETS FATHER CHRISTMAS

BY Enid Blyton

CONTENTS

Macdonald

"I'VE GOT SOME VERY EXCITING NEWS," SAID BIG-EARS

1

EXCITING NEWS

ONE morning Big-Ears came knocking at Noddy's little front door in great excitement.

"Noddy, are you in? Noddy, open the door!"

Noddy was in. He ran to the door at once. "Hello, Big-Ears. Have you come to ask me to tea?"

"No, but I've got some very exciting news," said Big-Ears. "Who do you think is coming next week? Guess!"

"I can't ever guess things, you know that, Big-Ears," said Noddy. "Quick, tell me!"

"Father Christmas!" said Big-Ears. "He's coming in his sleigh, with four reindeer. He's staying the night with my brother, Little-Ears."

"Goodness! What an honour!" said Noddy, feeling very excited too. "But why isn't he staying with *you*, Big-Ears?"

"Well, Little-Ears once lived at Father Christmas's Castle for a long time," said Big-Ears. "He's a wonderful packer and he used to pack Father Christmas's sack of toys for him. He could get thousands in that sack."

"Could he really?" said Noddy. "Dear me, why are we standing at the front door like this? Do come in and have a cup of cocoa, Big-Ears, and some biscuits. We must sit and talk some more about this exciting news. Shall I be able to see Father Christmas?"

"I hope so," said Big-Ears, going into Noddy's little house with him. "Dear me, your room isn't very tidy, little Noddy, not at all. I hope that you'll have everything just right before Father Christmas comes—and the garden looking nice as well. After all, Father Christmas is the King of Toyland, and a visit from him is really a most wonderful thing."

"DEAR ME! YOUR ROOM ISN'T VERY TIDY, NODDY"

"Yes. Yes, it is," said little Noddy, getting down the biscuit tin. "I'll have everything lovely, Big-Ears. And I'll polish my car till it's so bright that Father Christmas can use it for a mirror!"

They sat down and had some cocoa and biscuits. "My brother, Little-Ears, was very friendly indeed with Father Christmas," said Big-Ears. "He's very excited that Father Christmas wants to stay with him for a night. You see, once a year he takes his reindeer and goes through Toyland to look at the toys he gives to children."

"Oh—will we see him riding through our town in his sleigh?" said Noddy. "I shall get two very clean hankies and wave one in each hand as he goes by."

"Now listen," said Big-Ears. "I've thought of a great treat for you, little Noddy."

"What is it? Oh, you are *kind*, Big-Ears!" said Noddy, his head nodding madly.

"Well, my brother, Little-Ears, has asked me to supper on the night that Father Christmas is there," said Big-Ears, "and I thought you could take me in your car, Noddy. Then perhaps you might get a good look at Father Christmas!"

"Oh, Big-Ears! Oh, what a wonderful idea!" said Noddy, almost falling off his chair in excitement. "Oh, I'll make my car look simply beautiful. Oh, dear me!"

"I thought you'd be pleased," said Big-Ears, beaming at Noddy. "Well, you're a good little fellow, Noddy, and you work hard—so you deserve a treat."

"I'll wait outside in my car, and then take you safely home again," said Noddy.

"Thank you," said Big-Ears. "Now I must order myself a new suit with a cloak because I must be very grandly dressed if I'm to have supper with Father Christmas."

2

NODDY IS CLEVER

NODDY took Big-Ears to Miss Thimble Doll to be measured for a new cloak and a new suit. Miss Thimble was most excited to hear why Big-Ears was having a new suit.

"Is Noddy to have new clothes too?" she asked.

"No," said Big-Ears, "he isn't having supper with Father Christmas. But he's going to give his car a new coat of paint and shine it up till it's quite dazzling."

"Yes, I am," said Noddy. "What about your cat, Big-Ears?"

"It can have a grand new ribbon," said Big-Ears, "and perhaps a bow on its tail. Last time I had a party my cat tied six bows on its tail, but I think that's too many. Have you finished measuring me, Miss Thimble Doll?"

"Yes. You're a little bit plump, Mr Big-Ears," said Miss Thimble. "It's a pity, because I don't want your new suit to look tight."

"It isn't a pity," said Big-Ears. "My brother

Little-Ears is plump like me; and as for Father Christmas, he's so tubby that he shakes just like a jelly when he laughs. And very nice too!"

"Could I grow a bit plump too, Big-Ears?" asked Noddy. "I'd like to be like you."

"You wait till you're a hundred years old, like me!" said Big-Ears, laughing. "Now, have you finished, Miss Thimble Doll? Right. Please deliver everything on Tuesday of next week. My supper party is the next day. Good morning!"

Noddy was very, very busy for the next few days. He washed all his clothes, and went about in Mr Tubby's old dressing-gown till they were dry. Mrs Tubby, who lived next door, lent it to him. He really looked rather nice in it.

Mrs Tubby ironed Noddy's clean clothes for him, because she was afraid he might scorch them. She sewed on a button, too, and she bought him new blue laces for his shoes. He was very pleased.

"I don't expect Father Christmas will even *see* me," he said. "But I'll be all clean and tidy just in case he does, shan't I, Mrs Tubby Bear?"

Noddy painted his car beautifully in bright red and yellow. Then he polished it all over. Then

he polished it again, and the little car was most surpriscd.

"Parp-parp," it said, in a small voice.

"It's all right. I'm not going to sell you or give you to anyone," said Noddy, polishing away. "It's just because we are going to see a Most Important Person."

Noddy felt a song coming into his head that he could sing in time to his polishing. He began to sing very loudly indeed, and Mrs Tubby Bear came out to listen.

"OH...!
There's a Most Important Person
That I hope we're going to see,
With eyes that shine and twinkle
Just as brightly as the sea!

His beard is white as snow-flakes,
He wears a scarlet hood,
And all the children love him,
Because he's kind and good!
OH...!
This Most Important Person
That I hope we're going to see
Comes tumbling down the chimney
To visit you and me!
You surely know his name now,
So shout it loud and clear:
It's dear old FATHER CHRISTMAS,
And soon he will be here!"

Mrs Tubby simply couldn't help clapping after she heard this surprising song of little Noddy's. "I don't know how you think of your songs," she said.

"I *don't* think of them," said Noddy. "They just come into my head all ready to sing."

"Sing it again," said Mrs Tubby. "And I'll join in the 'OH!' part and I'll shout Father Christmas's name, too. Look, here's the Wobbly-Man—and here comes Miss Fluffy Cat with Mr Jumbo—and there's Mrs Noah and Sally Skittle. They've all heard you singing, Noddy, and they've come to listen. Sing away!"

"THEY'VE ALL HEARD YOU SINGING, NODDY!"

So Noddy took a deep breath and sang his song again. "OH...!" he began, and then, in time to his polishing, he sang it all through. His polishing helped everyone to sing, and you should just have heard them shout "FATHER CHRISTMAS" when the song came to his name.

Big-Ears was coming along on his bicycle, and when he heard the shout he almost fell off!

"Good gracious—what's that noise?" he said. "Why, there's little Noddy polishing his car, and everyone round him!"

So, of course, Big-Ears had to hear the song too and everyone sang it to him, with a very loud "OH!" and a very loud "FATHER CHRISTMAS" at the right time. It was wonderful.

"Why, Noddy!" said Big-Ears. "That really is marvellous. You can all stand outside Little-Ears' house and sing it to Father Christmas while he's having his supper inside with me and Little-Ears."

"Oh, no. It's just a silly song that came into my head, and sang itself in my mouth," said Noddy. But Big-Ears kept on saying that it really must be sung to Father Christmas.

"It's a polishing song, really," said Noddy. "It came because I was polishing."

"Oh, it can be sung without polishing," said Big-Ears, quite proud of little Noddy. "I've just been trying on my cloak, Noddy. It's fine. It drags behind me quite a long way."

"That's nothing," said Miss Fluffy Cat. "My tail *always* does that. I'm going to have it specially washed for Wednesday, and curled."

"I wish I could have *my* tail done like that," said Mr Jumbo. "But it hasn't got enough hairs. I shall have a bow right at the very top."

What fun everyone had getting ready for Father Christmas! There hadn't been such excitement in Toy Town for years!

3

HURRAH FOR FATHER CHRISTMAS!

WEDNESDAY came at last. It was a sunny day with little white clouds scattered about the sky, hardly moving. Everyone was up very early.

Noddy gave his car one last polish. It really looked magnificent, as good as new. He tied a big bow in front, in the middle of the bumper.

"Parp-parp-PARP!" hooted the car, pleased.

Noddy took off his overall and went to wash himself and dress. He had even polished up the bell on the top of his blue hat and it jingled gaily. "Jingle-jingle, dingle-ding!" it sang as Noddy moved about happily.

The roadway had to be cleared for Father Christmas's arrival, because the sleigh and the four reindeer took up rather a lot of room. Noddy put his car safely in the garage, but he left the door open so that the car could join in the excitement and hoot at the right time.

He went to stand at his gateway. Big-Ears came along on his bicycle, but he had kept to the side-roads in case Mr Plod the policeman turned him off the main road.

"Big-Ears, I'm glad you've come," said Noddy. "Oh, why haven't you got on your cloak?"

"That's for tonight," said Big-Ears. "Do you like my new suit, Noddy?"

"It's very, very grand," said Noddy, looking hard at Big-Ears. "It seems funny to see you in red, though. Still your hat is the same. Oh listen—the people are cheering down the road—and I can hear bells jing-jingling! It's FATHER CHRISTMAS coming!"

So it was. Noddy began to dance about with excitement and he trod on Big-Ears' feet, but Big-Ears was so excited that he didn't even notice it.

The noise of the bells grew louder and louder. "JING-JING-JING-JINGLE-JING! JINGLE-JING!"

And then Noddy saw the reindeer coming up the road. How lovely they looked with their great antlers growing from their heads! JING-JING-JINGLE-JING.

And there was Father Christmas in his sleigh, smiling all over his big red face, his blue eyes twinkling all the time. He waved his hand to everyone, and his red cloak flew out in the wind behind him.

JING-JING-JINGLE-JING. Hurrah, hurrah, hurrah! Good old Father Christmas, hurrah, hurrah, hurrah! Long live Father Christmas, hurrah, hurrah, JING-JING-JINGLE-JING!

What a noise of cheering and jingling—and then Noddy's little car joined in with excited hoots. "PARP-PARP-PARP!" It even ran out of its garage right up behind Noddy and Big-Ears, but they didn't notice it.

Father Christmas passed by, waving and smiling—then he and his reindeer were gone. Noddy gave a big sigh. "I like him. I do, do like

HURRAH! GOOD OLD FATHER CHRISTMAS

him. I wish I could speak to him. I wish I could do something for him."

Big-Ears laughed. "Well, you may get a peep at him tonight, but that's all, little Noddy. You certainly won't be able to speak to him, or do anything for him. He's a Most Important Person, you know."

"Yes, I do know. It's what my song says," said little Noddy, his head nodding up and down. "I'm glad my song is going to be sung outside Little-Ears' house tonight. Father Christmas won't know it's my song, but *I* shall."

"Now, you call for me at half-past six EXACTLY," said Big-Ears to Noddy. "And I'll show you how my cloak looks, and then you can drive me to my brother Little-Ears. He has a toadstool house like mine, but much bigger."

"I'll be there," promised Noddy. "Oh, isn't this a most exciting day, Big-Ears. I think I can feel another song coming."

"Not now, Noddy—you really must do some work," said Big-Ears, getting on his bicycle. "Goodbye. See you later."

4

OFF TO LITTLE-EARS'

NODDY was ready in good time that evening. Mrs Tubby came to see if he looked clean and tidy before he left. She pulled his yellow scarf straight, and looked behind his ears to see if he had washed them. He had.

"You'll do, little Noddy," she said. "Have you got a clean hanky in your pocket?"

"Oooh no—I quite forgot!" said Noddy and rushed to get one. "Wouldn't it be dreadful if I had to sneeze into a dirty hanky just as Father Christmas looked at me?"

"It certainly would," said Mrs Tubby. "There—you look very nice." She gave him a kiss and he got into his car, which shone so brightly that Mrs Tubby could hardly bear to look at it!

Noddy drove to Big-Ears' toadstool house in the wood. He hooted outside, "Parp-parp!"

Big-Ears looked out of the window. "Come in and see my new cloak!" he said.

Noddy went in. There stood Big-Ears in his new suit, and behind him, hanging from his shoulders, was a fine crimson cloak.

"Goodness me—you DO look grand!" said

Noddy, beaming. "I feel very proud of you, Big-Ears. Why don't you wear a cloak always?"

"I fall over it rather," said Big-Ears. "And it would get very muddy if I wore it out-of-doors. Well, I'm ready!"

He walked out of his toadstool house, his cloak coming grandly behind him. But in the little garden it caught on a bramble and Big-Ears had to stop and undo it. Then it caught on a bit of wire and this time Noddy had to undo it.

"I think I'll pick it up and carry it to the car," said Big-Ears, impatiently. "I hope it's not going to behave like this all the time."

Off they went—but as soon as they got into the wind the cloak blew out behind the car and flapped like a red sail! How all the rabbits stared when the car passed! Big-Ears was very glad when they came to Little-Ears' house. "Here we are!" he said. "Noddy, isn't Little-Ears' toadstool house a beauty?"

Noddy stared at it. It really was the biggest toadstool he had ever seen.

"Little-Ears rubbed a bit of Grow-Big Magic on it," said Big-Ears. "It's very comfortable inside."

"Where are the reindeer?" asked Noddy. "Oh, I can see them. They're tied to the trees over there. I can hear their bells jingling too."

"Now, you wait outside Little-Ears' house till I come out after dinner to go home," said Big-Ears. "You might *just* catch sight of Father Christmas looking out of the window."

"When is my song going to be sung?" asked Noddy, anxiously. "You haven't forgotten about that, have you?"

"Of course not," said Big-Ears. "Mr Tubby Bear and some others of his very good friends are coming at eight-thirty to sing it for you. You can stand in front of them all and conduct them."

"What's conducting?" asked Noddy in fright. "I can't conduct. That's what people on buses do."

"ISN'T LITTLE-EARS' HOUSE A BEAUTY?"

"You're thinking of bus-conductors, you silly little fellow!" said Big-Ears, laughing. "You just beat time, that's all—like this!"

"Oh—that's easy," said Noddy. "Let me help you out, Big-Ears. Your cloak is tangled up. Shall I walk behind you and hold it up till you get to the front door?"

"Oh yes—that would look very grand," said Big-Ears, so Noddy held up his crimson cloak beautifully for him as he walked proudly to the door. Little-Ears opened it. He was very like Big-Ears, but his ears were not so large. He beamed at little Noddy. "Hallo! Pleased to see you. Come in, Big-Ears. Father Christmas is waiting."

Big-Ears went inside and the door was shut. Noddy gave a big sigh. How he would have liked to go inside too, and sit in a little dark corner and listen to Father Christmas talking. But he was only

little Noddy, a funny little fellow with a nodding head. He wasn't important at all.

He went back to his car and got inside. He would wait till the others came to sing his song.

He kept his eyes on the nearby window of Little-Ears' house, but he didn't see Father Christmas looking out. It was very disappointing.

At half-past eight he heard the others coming and he got out of the car. Ah—now he would conduct them! He would beat time while they sang his song. He would *feel* important even if he wasn't!

5

FATHER CHRISTMAS IS KIND

MR TUBBY arranged the singers in a row. Noddy stood in front, suddenly feeling very shy. Everyone looked at him, and Noddy raised a little twig he had found in a ditch.

"OH . . .!" sang everyone, and then went on with the song.

> "There's a Most Important Person
> That I hope we're going to see . . ."

Right on to the end of the song they all went, and you should have heard how they shouted out Father Christmas's name when they came to it in the song!

The door opened—and out came the Most Important Person himself! He smiled round at

everyone and his blue eyes twinkled brightly.

"Very nice indeed," he said. "And may I ask which of you wrote that extremely good song?"

"Noddy did," said Miss Fluffy, and she pushed Noddy towards Father Christmas. "He's our taxi-driver and he often makes up songs."

"Dear me—so *this* is little Noddy!" said Father Christmas and smiled such a big smile that Noddy felt warm all over. Father Christmas put out his hand and Noddy shook it, very red in the face.

"So you're a taxi-driver, are you?" said Father Christmas. "Where's your car?"

"Here," said Noddy, finding his tongue, and waved his hand towards his little car.

"Parp-parp," said the car, and put its lights on and off all by itself.

"What a *dear* little car!" said Father Christmas. "And how beautifully clean and shiny! Dear me, I wish I could travel through Toyland in this instead of going in my bumpy old sleigh. It's such a nuisance too, having to find a stable each night for my four reindeer."

"Oh," said Noddy, going even redder than ever. "O Most Important Person, please have my car while you are here in Toyland. It's very easy to drive."

"WHAT A DEAR LITTLE CAR," SAID FATHER CHRISTMAS

"That's kind of you," said Father Christmas, "but it would be a change for me to be driven instead of driving myself. I suppose you wouldn't like to come with me and drive me where I want to go?"

Noddy lost his tongue again. He couldn't say a single word! He just stared at Father Christmas as if he couldn't believe his ears.

Big-Ears spoke up then, feeling very excited. "Father Christmas, sir, little Noddy's lost for words because he's so pleased—but of course he'll drive you anywhere you want to go. He'll be here at nine o'clock tomorrow morning, won't you, Noddy?"

Noddy's head nodded so fast that it made Father Christmas quite giddy to look at him. He laughed, patted Noddy on the shoulder and went back into Little-Ears' house.

"Oh," said Noddy, sitting down suddenly. "Oh! I must be dreaming!" But he wasn't—it was quite, quite true!

6

A DRIVE WITH FATHER CHRISTMAS

NEXT morning Noddy was outside Little-Ears' house at exactly nine o'clock. Out came Father Christmas. He was always very punctual. He smiled at Noddy and got into the car beside him. It was a bit of a squash, because Father Christmas was very plump indeed.

"Now, let me see," said Father Christmas, taking out a fat notebook. "I want to go to Bouncing Ball Village. I hear that some of the balls I gave to children last year hadn't got much bounce in them. I must inquire into that."

Off they went, Noddy feeling as proud as could be. His bell jingled all the time.

"You sound like a small reindeer, jingling like that!" said Father Christmas, and gave one of his enormous laughs.

After that Noddy couldn't be shy. He talked to Father Christmas and told him all about himself—how he had been made by an old man called Mr Carver and how he had been lonely and had run away from him to Toyland.

"And now I've got a little house and a garage and this car—and lots of friends," said Noddy, happily.

"Ah, a lot of friends—that's very important," said Father Christmas. "Hallo—are we in Bouncing

Ball Village so soon? Good. Call the Chief Bouncer to me, will you?''

Little balls came bouncing round to see who had come. When they saw it was Father Christmas they bounced in excitement, trying to jump right over the car.

The Chief Bouncer was an enormous coloured ball, the kind that likes to be played with at the seaside. He listened to Father Christmas's complaints, and then, in a queer bouncing kind of voice, he promised to see that every ball in the village should have proper bouncing lessons before being sent to the world of boys and girls.

''Now go to Teddy Town,'' said Father Christmas. ''I've had very good reports from boys and girls about their teddy bears—they love them very much. I want to give some praise there.''

THE CHIEF BOUNCER WAS AN ENORMOUS COLOURED BALL

On they went to Teddy Town. The Chief Teddy was very proud to see Father Christmas.

"You are training your teddy bears well," said Father Christmas. "I am pleased with you. One little girl has asked for a tiny doll's house teddy bear. Can you do anything about that?"

"Certainly, Father Christmas," said the Chief Teddy. "Pray come in for some lemonade."

"No, thank you," said Father Christmas. "I have a lot to do today. On to Rocking-Horse Town, please, Noddy."

So on they went, and the little car behaved beautifully. It didn't knock any lamp-posts down, it didn't go into puddles, and it ran round bumps in the road instead of jolting over them.

"Very comfortable car, this," said Father Christmas. "Ah—here's a rocking-horse coming full-tilt at us. Whoa, there—look where you're going!"

7

EVERYTHING IS VERY EXCITING

THE rocking-horse rocked by at top speed, amazed to see Father Christmas in the little car. It soon spread the news, and a great many rocking-horses, big and small, came rocking up.

"Hrrrumph!" said a great big one, spotted all over, with a very fine, swishy tail. "Father

Christmas, I am honoured to see you. I hope that you are wanting as many of us as ever?"

"Oh, dear me, yes," said Father Christmas. "The children are just as fond of rocking-horses as ever they were. But I want smaller ones than I used to have, please. People haven't got room for the enormous ones now."

"Very well, sir," said the big rocking-horse.

It was a very exciting day. Noddy felt so proud to be driving Father Christmas. He felt prouder still to sit at a table and have tea with him, and he was very pleased to find that Father Christmas liked ice-creams as much as he did!

They slept in Humming-Top Village that night, and all night long there was the humming of excited tops who couldn't go to sleep because Father Christmas had come to visit them.

"It's quite a nice sound, Father Christmas," said Noddy, sleepily. "Like a lot of bees humming in the flowers. Oh dear me—I'm so sleepy!"

Next day off they went again. They went to Wooden-Engine Village, and Noddy had time to leave his car and go and drive one. He had always wanted to do that. Look at him—he's really driving the engine much too fast! Look out, Father Christmas, look out!

LOOK OUT, FATHER CHRISTMAS, LOOK OUT!

They drove off to Doll's-house Town and Noddy thought the little houses were lovely. Tiny little dolls ran out to cheer Father Christmas.

"I've just come to say that some of you dolls who go to live in doll's-houses in the playrooms of boys and girls are not very good at housework," said Father Christmas. "You don't know how to dust or scrub floors or clean windows. Well, you must learn, please."

"Yes, Father Christmas," the tiny dolls cried. "We'll learn, we promise we will."

Then they went on to Skittle Town; and dear me, what a shock for Noddy when he saw all the skittles lining up right in front of his car. He jammed on his brakes at once.

"No, drive into them," said Father Christmas. "Skittles are made to be knocked down, and it will be such fun for them."

So Noddy drove full speed into the squealing skittles. Down they fell, laughing away like anything!

"And now," said Father Christmas, "I want to go to a place I haven't been to before—a small place called N. & B. Works. What in the world do N. and B. stand for? I know it's something to do with perfectly new toys—but WHAT can they be? N. and B.—most peculiar!"

8

A SURPRISE FOR LITTLE NODDY

FATHER CHRISTMAS asked the way to the N. & B. Works, and a shy little toy bunny told him. "Down there and over the hill. They're making new toys. The children asked for them."

Noddy drove on and soon they came to a small factory built rather like a little castle. "Drive to the front, then stop and hoot," said Father Christmas. "The new toys will come running out and I'll have a look at them. If I don't like them I won't take them to the children for Christmas."

Noddy stopped his little car outside the building and hooted loudly. "Parp-parp-parp!" What do

you THINK? Out poured
dozens and dozens of tiny little Noddy and Big-Ears dolls! Yes, really!

Noddy couldn't believe his eyes. Why, they were exactly like him, but much smaller—and all dressed like him too!

"The Noddies have even got bells on their blue hats like me," said Noddy, amazed. "And the Big-Ears have red hats and beards just like *my* Big-Ears!"

"N. & B. Works—of course, Noddy and Big-Ears Works!" said Father Christmas. "I see that the children have asked for Noddy and Big-Ears toys, Noddy. I wonder why."

"Well, there are lots of books about me," said Noddy. "Perhaps they have read them. Oh, Father Christmas— OH, Father Christmas—when I see all these little toys *just* like me I feel Very, Very Important!"

"Now don't you be too grand and important or you won't be the dear little Noddy that children love," said Father Christmas. He looked closely at the tiny figures running excitedly round the car. "Yes, I like them. Pity the Noddies haven't little cars like yours, Noddy. I'll have to make a note of that."

"Jingle-jingle-jing!" went the tiny little bells on the hats of the tiny little Noddies.

"JINGLE-JINGLE-JINGLE-JING!" said Noddy's big bell, loudly and proudly.

"Can we have a ride?" called the little figures, and they clambered all over the car.

"Just for a little way," said Father Christmas. "Drive on, Noddy, and give them a ride!"

There they go: Noddy's car covered with tiny Noddies just like himself, and little Big-Ears with beards and red hats. Well, well, well!

THERE GOES NODDY'S LITTLE CAR COVERED WITH TINY NODDIES

9

THE WONDERFUL PARTY

NODDY was very sorry when it was time to go home. He *had* enjoyed himself with Father Christmas. He loved the kind, jolly old man—and it seemed as if Father Christmas loved him too.

"We'll have a party when we get back," he said to Noddy. "I feel like a party, Noddy. Do you?"

"Oh, yes—I *always* feel like a party—just like I *always* feel like an ice-cream," said Noddy. "Dear me—what a lot I shall have to tell Big-Ears when I get home!"

Big-Ears was very pleased to see Noddy safely home again and to hear from Father Christmas what a splendid little driver he had been. He gave Noddy such a hug that Noddy couldn't breathe for quite a long time, and gasped like a goldfish out of water!

"We're going to have a party," said Noddy. "Will you and Little-Ears arrange it, Big-Ears?"

"You shall have one tomorrow!" said Big-Ears, beaming. "In the market-place, so that everyone can come. I'll get the big town-bell and go and call out the news."

So there goes old Big-Ears, beaming all over his face, ringing the bell as loudly as ever he can. "DINGA-DONG! DINGA-DONG! News! NEWS! NEWS!"

Well, it wasn't long before everyone heard the news that Father Christmas and little Noddy were safely back and were going to have a party. Goodness me, what excitement there was!

"It will be one of the finest parties ever!" said Big-Ears. "And I shall wear my red cloak again. I shall tie it round my waist if I keep falling over it."

The reindeer were asked to the party, too, and Little-Ears spent a long time polishing their antlers for them. In fact, everyone was asked, even the bunnies in the woods.

The party began at three o'clock, and there was so much to eat that the tables that stood in the middle of the market-place creaked under the

THE PARTY BEGAN AT THREE O'CLOCK

weight of it all.

Father Christmas sat at the top of the table and Noddy sat on his right-hand side, feeling so proud that he could hardly speak a word. His bell rang all the time, though, and his little car, parked nearby, hooted.

"Jingle-parp, PARP-jingle-jing, parple, parple-parple, jingle-jing!" What a noise!

Father Christmas got up and made a speech. "I don't make long speeches," he said, "but I do want to say that Noddy is one of the nicest, kindest little toys I've ever met, and QUITE the best driver!"

"Hooray! Hooray!" cried everyone.

"Speech, Noddy, speech!" shouted Mr and Mrs Tubby. Noddy began to tremble.

Big-Ears pushed him to his feet.

"I don't know what to say," said little Noddy. "I—I don't—know—" And then suddenly he stood up straight and smiled.

"It's all right!" he said "I'll sing a song instead!"

And here is the song that he sang at that wonderful party:

"I'm only little Noddy
Who's got a song to sing,
And a little car to ride in,
And a bell to jingle-jing.
I've a little house to live in
And a little garage too.
But I've something BIG inside me,
And that's my love for YOU -
My love for ALL of you!"

Much better than a speech, little Noddy. No wonder everyone is clapping and cheering you. Well done!

All Noddy books are available at your bookshop or newsagent, or can be ordered from the following address: Noddy Enterprises, Cash Sales Department, P.O. Box 11, Falmouth, Cornwall, TR10 9EN.

For all orders (U.K., Overseas, Eire or B.F.P.O.) please send cheque or postal order (no currency), and allow 60p for postage and packing for the first book plus 20p for the second book and 20p for each additional book ordered up to a maximum charge of £2.00.